2006

Many Blessings to You!
Enjoy! - Dawn Anderson

Chimpanzee, Like Me !

By Dawn Anderson

Opposable Thumb Press

Chimpanzee, Like Me !
Copyright © 2006
Text and Illustrations by Dawn Anderson
Printed in the U.S.A. All rights reserved, including the right of reproduction in whole or in part in any form.

Published by

Opposable Thumb Press
P.O. Box 409107, Chicago, IL 60640-9107

www.opposablethumbpress.com

ISBN 13 978-0-9786570-0-0
ISBN 10 0-9786570-0-4
1 2 3 4 5 6 7 8 9 10
First Edition

Typesetting in Myraid Std, Nueva Std , Marker Felt and Minion Pro
Printed and bound by Lake Book Manufacturing, Inc., Melrose Park, Illinois
Prepress done by Anthology
Cover jackets done by Lehigh Lithographers, Inc.

Dedicated to
the Evelyns (Anderson and Johnson),
who brought my family into the world,
and to
Gloria and Allen, who brought me into the world.

Special Thanks to:

David Meyer, Jane O'Donnell, Myrna Hasse and Barb Beitz for the education in publishing; Sue Shekut for the education in business and self-confidence; my friends at Lincoln Park Zoo for the education in zoos: the Spanish translation team - Rose Lambert and Pilar Baltierra, with help from Mark Wehling and J Nikolas Nava; and especially, Lehigh Lithographers and Mike Mueller for their generosity in producing the dust jackets. Finally, my gratitude for the inspiration that is the life of Jane Goodall.

I'm very excited today. My mom and I are at the zoo, and I get to meet one of the zoo babies. My mom works at the zoo, so I don't get to just *see* the baby. I get to *meet* him ! His name is Berundi, and he is a baby chimpanzee.

Berundi is almost two years old, the same as my baby brother.

My name is Madeline and I'm four. Even though Berundi is younger than me, we are a lot alike. Berundi has been growing up a lot just like me and my baby brother.

The chimpanzees live in a really big room with lots of ropes and trees. There's a door where they can go outside to another big space, just like my yard outside at home. People who visit the zoo get to see them in these places.

But at the back of the big room there's another place visitors don't see. Behind a special door is another room, and only people who work at the zoo (like my mom), can go there.

Berundi's family is the same size as mine. I live with my mom, dad, baby brother, and grandma and grandpa. Berundi lives with his mom, dad, older sister, and his aunt and cousin. Berundi has grandparents too, but they live in another zoo.

It's lunchtime at the zoo and my mom is setting up the food for Berundi and his family. They eat lots of vegetables and fruit, and even get a little milk and "monkey chow," which looks like little cookies. They also eat tiny worms called grubs.

If Berundi's family lived in the jungle they would eat lots of plants and bugs (called termites), in the same way that people eat vegetables and sometimes, meat.

The chimpanzees know when it is time to eat, and they wait by the special door to meet my mom. When Berundi's mom gets to the food she picks up a banana and starts to peel it.

Even though they are big and long, her hands look a lot like mine, and she peels a banana the same way I do.

She very carefully picks up a grub and shows it to Berundi. He smells it, then eats it. Then he takes the banana peel and throws it on his head. My mom and I start laughing. Then he scrunches up his mouth and lips and sounds like he is laughing too.

When Berundi laughs he makes quiet hee-hee-hee noises.

I try to go up to the special door, but my mom keeps me away from it. She says chimpanzees can get sick with the same things that we do, and she doesn't want me to spread germs to Berundi and his family. So I stand away from the door.

Berundi is done playing with the banana peel.
He looks at his mom, who is looking out toward
the crowds of visitors at the zoo. Then he slowly
creeps near the door. He looks at me and I look at
him.

I make a funny face .... and he makes one back.

Then he does another.....

....and another.

We move our faces in the same way, and we both like to play by making funny faces.

But Berundi is done with the fun and decides to go play closer to his mom.

Berundi pulls himself up on a rope, then hangs from a branch and watches us.

Chimpanzees mostly walk using both their arms and legs. They use their long arms to climb trees, and their toes to hold onto things. Their arms are very, very strong. Chimpanzees are stronger than even my dad. My arms are shorter than a chimpanzee, but I like to climb trees too.

Later today the chimpanzees will need to go to sleep, just like I will. When they go to sleep at night, the chimpanzees don't have their own bedrooms, but they make beds for themselves every night.

If they lived in the jungle, their beds would be up in the trees, and made of branches.

Just like I watch and copy what I see my parents do, Berundi watches his family to learn to do the things chimpanzees do. He has to learn what it means to be nice and to be a part of his family, just like me.

Sometimes it is very easy to learn what to do, and sometimes it is very fun. And sometimes, both Berundi and I have to sit down and think about why it is important to be nice and be part of a family.

It is time for us to go home and eat our lunch, so my mom and I walk away from the special door. Berundi comes back towards us and makes a quiet "ou-ou-ou" sound.

Then he lifts both arms to say goodbye. I raise my hand and wave goodbye to my new friend.

Chimp Info Page

Most people get to first meet chimpanzees at the zoo. We learn a lot about chimpanzees and humans from what we see chimps do in zoos. But it is from watching how chimpanzees live in the wild that we learn the most, and zoos use that information to improve the lives of the chimps they care for. Here are a few points about why it is important that chimpanzees remain living in the wild, and why it is useful for people to learn from chimps in zoos.

Family Groups – Central Africa is the only place where chimpanzees live in the wild. We know that chimps live in large extended family groups that usually have an adult male as leader. Chimps take several years to mature, and it is important that the mother and greater family be there to teach young chimps how to survive. People have the same need to teach our children over time, how to survive, and we've learned that the way people organize themselves at work or in politics or in families, is similar to chimpanzee social structure.

Health and Medicine – Chimpanzee health is similar to human health. In zoos, veterinarians monitor and care for the animals, and they are constantly learning new ways to promote health, just like doctors do for humans. Wild chimps know what plants to eat to help with a lot of their illnesses. By watching them, we learn about new resources for treating our own health problems. In this way, chimpanzees teach humans about good medicine.

Food – For wild chimpanzees, collecting and sharing food is a very important part of social behavior and survival. People have many celebrations, rituals and routines built around food. By observing wild chimpanzees, especially in situations where food is involved, we learn more about our own human nature. For example, we once thought that tool use was part of what sets us apart from other animals. But when we discovered that chimpanzees use basic tools to fish for termites, we had to think again about what makes humans unique.

Communication – Chimps lack the physical throat structure to speak like people, but in captivity, they have shown that they understand spoken human language, and symbolic picture images and sign language. Chimpanzees use facial expressions and body language and gestures in very similar ways that people do. What we observe in wild and captive apes (which include chimps, gorillas and orangutans) helps us to understand the many ways people communicate without using words.